SHERLOCK SAM

SHER SAM

By A.J. LOW

Andrews McMeel Publishing®

a division of Andrews McMeel Universal

Epigram Books Pte. Ltd.
1008 Toa Payoh North #03-08 Singapore 318996
Tel: +65 6292 4456 / Fax: +65 6292 4414
enquiry@epigrambooks.sg / www.epigrambooks.sg

Andrews McMeel Publishing
a division of Andrews McMeel Universal
1130 Walnut Street, Kansas City, Missouri 64106

www.andrewsmcmeel.com

17 18 19 20 21 SDB 10 9 8 7 6 5 4 3 2 1

ISBN: 978-1-4494-7975-6

Library of Congress Number: 2016944858

Made by:
Shenzhen Donnelley Printing Company Ltd.
Address and location of manufacturer:
No. 47, Wuhe Nan Road, Bantian Ind. Zone,
Shenzhen China, 518129
1st Printing—11/21/16

FOR THE OCTOPUSES:
Wherever in the world you all may be

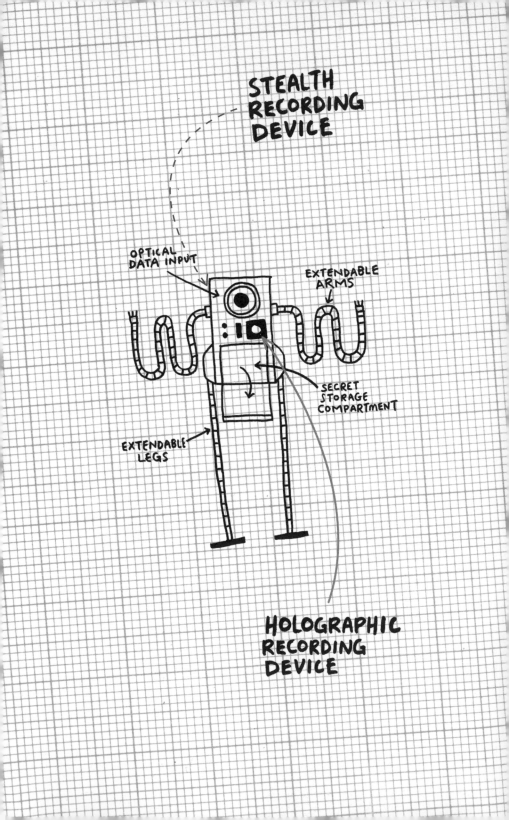

STEALTH
RECORDING
DEVICE

OPTICAL
DATA INPUT

EXTENDABLE
ARMS

SECRET
STORAGE
COMPARTMENT

EXTENDABLE
LEGS

HOLOGRAPHIC
RECORDING
DEVICE

CHAPTER ONE

"Everything-has-gone-black," Watson said.

"It'll only be for a second," I replied, squinting in concentration.

I was standing in front of my robot, putting the finishing touches on the new equipment I had just added to him. Unfortunately, a side effect of my tinkering meant that Watson would lose his vision function for a short while. Needless to say, he didn't take to that kindly.

"It-has-been-twelve-seconds-and-everything-is-still-black," Watson said.

I pushed a button.

"My-vision-has-returned," Watson reported. "You-have-been-eating-biscuits-in-bed-again. I-see-crumbs."

I made a mental note to install a vacuuming function in Watson. Then instead of just complaining, he could help curb the constant crumb situation that infested my bedroom.

"We'll test out your new superpower tonight, Watson! But for now, dinner!" I said. "I smell . . ."

I paused and sniffed the air.

"Bacon!" I cried.

Dragging Watson by the arm, I dashed out of my bedroom.

"Three, two, one . . . A-HA!" Wendy exclaimed as I entered the dining room. She was holding a crisp slice of bacon and waving it in

the air. My sister can be very strange at times.

"Aha, what?" I said, taking my seat. Wait, the dinner table was empty! Where was dinner?

"I was just testing a theory. Dad and you aren't the only ones who experiment," Wendy replied, snickering. She popped the slice of bacon in her mouth and chewed. "Mom said dinner will be ready in five minutes, by the way."

A trap! I had been lured to the dinner table by a bacon-waving sister!

"I-believe-this-time-it-is-Wendy-one-Sherlock-zero," Watson said.

I glared at my robot as I walked to the kitchen to see if I could help Mom.

Dad was already there, carefully putting the cooked slices of bacon on top of lettuce, cucumber, tomato, and cheese. Mom had grilled the bread so that the cheese was melted to perfection, just the way I liked it! She was putting the finishing touches on her potato salad—bacon bits! I helped carry everything to the dinner table quickly.

"No sneaking extra helpings of bacon, Sam!" Mom called out from the kitchen. Mom is a great cook, but I am never allowed extra helpings of anything, except vegetables.

Wendy grinned at me widely as I sat down. I frowned at her in return. She pulled out a slice of bacon from her sandwich and waved it about. But before I could inform Mom about Wendy's devious ploy, she put it on my plate, right on top of my sandwich, and smiled.

Sometimes, having a big sister is pretty nice.

I grinned back and quickly popped the bacon into my mouth before Mom caught us.

Dad, Mom, and Watson finally sat down as well.

"So, Sam, what's this letter game I hear people are playing?" Dad asked. "I read about it in the papers. The reporter called it a massive island-wide game of Chain Mail."

"It's not a game, Dad. It's a sociological experiment," I replied. Dad is a genius engineer and loves science; he understands the importance of experiments.

"Yes, of course, son. Could you explain this sociological experiment to your old dad?" he said, smiling.

"Basically, you receive letters from people all around Singapore with instructions on how to send out your own letter to another person," I said. "We have to use paper and pen, and snail mail. Sometimes it's your friends who send you letters, but they're not supposed to let you know."

"Oh! That's like the game we used to play when we were kids," Mom said. "This was long before email was invented. No one writes letters anymore. Such a pity."

"We're not playing it, Mom. We're participating in an experiment," I said.

"Yes, dear," Mom replied. She and Dad grinned at each other.

"For our game, I mean, experiment," Wendy said before I could correct her, "Sam and I wrote about our favorite books."

"Yeah! Then we mailed our letters to someone else with instructions for them to do the same," I said.

"How did you kids get involved in this experiment?" Dad asked.

"Nazhar was the first to receive a letter. And then later on, Wendy, Jimmy, and I—and even Watson—received letters, too!" I said. My initial reaction had been to try to track down the sender. It was a mystery! It had to be solved!

But Nazhar convinced me that not knowing who sent the letters was an important part of the experiment, and that by seeking him or her out, I would be ruining the experiment. It was logical, so I stopped my search.

"Wow!" Dad said. He turned excitedly to Mom and asked, "I wonder if we'll receive any chain letters?"

"I hope so," Mom replied. She looked just as excited as Dad. Mom loves to read and talk with Dad about the books she's read.

"May I have just one more slice of bacon?" I asked hopefully.

"No more bacon, Sam. But if you're still hungry, I can make you a tuna sandwich," Mom replied.

"Er, no thanks, Mom," I replied. Tuna. Always with the tuna.

Later that evening, at 9:30 p.m., I sent Watson to the kitchen to test out his new ability. I instructed him to come back to the room at

10:30 with his findings and double chocolate Khong Guan biscuits (if the coast was clear).

At 10:32 p.m., Watson returned to our room.

I immediately asked him for the most important thing.

"Did you get the double chocolate biscuits?" I said.

"No. Someone-came-to-the-kitchen-while-I-was-there," Watson said.

"Was it Dad sneaking ice cream again?" I asked. "No, wait, don't tell me. SHOW me!"

I ran over to turn the bedroom lights off.

With a soft whirring sound, Watson's tummy started to glow and a beam of light shot out from him. The new holographic projector I had installed in him earlier in the evening worked!

I saw a small, fuzzy image (I would have to recalibrate the projector later). However, the scene that Watson was playing back showed an empty kitchen.

"There's no one there, Watson," I said.

"Patience-is-a-virtue-of-aspiring-young-detectives," Watson replied.

I watched a few moments more, wondering what exactly would reward my patience.

Suddenly, I saw what Watson was referring to. Someone had entered the dark kitchen. The sneaking figure was walking on tiptoe and kept looking behind its shoulder, checking to see if anyone was following it. I immediately deduced that it didn't want anyone to know it was in the kitchen, or else it would have turned the light on! I shifted closer to the holographic image to get a better look. It had to be Dad. He knew Mom had a "No snacks after 10 p.m." rule. The figure reached up to the top shelf and took out the tin of Khong Guan biscuits! MY Khong Guan biscuits!

"It has to be Dad!" I exclaimed.

Just then, the dark figure walked over to the kitchen table to open the tin. The moonlight from the window hit its face.

"MOM?" I said. I turned to Watson, pointed at my holographic mother, and exclaimed in shock, "It's MOM! MOM is sneaking Khong Guan biscuits! MOM!"

"So-it-appears," Watson replied.

I was too surprised to do anything, but the last thing I remembered thinking before I fell asleep was . . . I wonder what Mom's favorite Khong Guan biscuit is.

ooo

CHAPTER TWO

"So, Mom, how did you sleep last night?"
I asked Mom as she drove Wendy, Watson,
and me to our lunch appointment. It was
Saturday and we were on our way to meet
Officer Siva for lunch at Albert Centre, a really
big hawker center along Queen Street, behind
Bugis Street.

"Me? I slept fine, Sam. Thank you for
asking," Mom replied, not taking her eyes off
the road.

Fine? A likely story! If I were Mom, I would have been riddled with guilt and unable to sleep all night long! I scrambled forward in my seat and searched Mom's face closely for clues, but her eyes were as unlined and clear as ever, with not a hint of any dark eye circles.

"Sam, what are you doing? Sit back down and buckle your seat belt properly," Mom scolded.

Wendy, who was seated in the front seat next to Mom, turned around and gave me a weird look.

"Do you know why Officer Siva wants to meet us, Sam?" Wendy asked.

"He said he wanted to thank us for helping him solve the Case of the Ghostly Moans," I replied, buckling my seat belt.

"Well, don't give Officer Siva too much trouble. I'll be shopping at my favorite bookstore at Bugis Junction, so just call me when you're done, okay?" Mom said.

"Yes, Mom," Wendy and I replied.

The hawker center was very crowded, but Officer Siva had already reserved a table for us. It was the first time we were seeing Officer Siva in something other than his police uniform. He looked much younger in a purple Transformers T-shirt and jeans.

"Hello, everyone! Hi, Mrs. Tan! Thanks for bringing the kids out to meet me on the weekend. Hope it wasn't jammed all the way," Officer Siva said.

"It's no problem at all. Thank you for treating the kids to lunch," Mom replied. "You really don't have to."

"Officer Siva, I'd like some black carrot cake and chicken rice, please!" I said cheerfully.

I had read reviews online that said Guan Kee's black carrot cake was super delicious.

"I'd like a bowl of fish ball noodles, please," Wendy said politely.

"I-would-like-some-used-batteries-please,"

Watson said. Used batteries are Watson's main source of power. He is an environmentally friendly robot.

"Kids, behave yourselves now!" Mom warned, but she was smiling as she left.

Officer Siva bought food for Wendy and me and pulled out a bag of used batteries from his backpack.

"When I called your mom to ask if I could buy you lunch, she told me that both your classes would be taking part in your school's first exchange program with an international school." Officer Siva said.

"Yes, we'll be attending Enterprise International School for a week. The school's nearby, along Queen Street," I said, digging into the piping hot plate of black carrot cake. I much prefer black carrot cake to white carrot cake because it is sweeter due to the sweet black sauce. The uncle at the stall had expertly mixed the egg into the carrot cake and the result was crispy gooey perfection!

"Both our classes are going. We were selected because we earned the most points for volunteering and doing good deeds in our community," Wendy said.

"Now I'll get to learn about what people from other countries like to eat," I said. "I wonder if they have special kinds of food at the school canteen!" Mom had even promised to give me pocket money instead of the usual packed lunches!

"*Wah*, that's a very interesting way to get kids involved in the community," Officer Siva said.

"Nazhar and Jimmy will be coming with us as well," I said, just in case Officer Siva didn't know that Jimmy was in my class and Nazhar was in Wendy's.

"And Eliza, too," Wendy said as she made a face. Wendy didn't like her classmate very much, because Eliza could be a bully. But even

Eliza had pitched in to earn good-deed points for her class.

"A friend of mine has a son who goes to Enterprise International School," Officer Siva said.

"Is your friend *ang moh*?" Wendy asked.

"Ha ha, yes, but his *moh* isn't *ang*. Though I think he secretly would like to be a redhead. His hair is as dark as yours and mine. He's actually from Mexico but his family lived in the U.S. for many years before he came to Singapore," Officer Siva replied. "His name is Fidel Alvarado. Have you kids heard of him?"

"Oh! I've heard of him. He wrote that children's book about the boy who thought he was a superhero," Wendy said. She turned and looked at me just as she said it.

"And it was adapted into a comic as well. Dad bought it for me," I replied, taking a spoonful of my chicken rice. It was tasty, but Mom's chicken rice was much more delicious.

"That's him. We drink *kopi* at the same *kopitiam* every morning, and after a while, we became friends. I taught him how to order *kopi* properly, Singapore style! And he taught me Spanish," Officer Siva said.

"How do you say *kopi* in Spanish, Officer Siva?" Wendy asked.

"*Café!*" Officer Siva replied, grinning widely. "Fidel's son Luis is in the fourth grade at Enterprise International School. But recently, Fidel has been thinking of removing him from the school and going back to the U.S.," Officer Siva said.

"Why does he want to leave? Is it because of durian?" I asked. I love durian and can never figure out why people say it is stinky. I especially love durian pengat.

"They actually love durian, Sherlock," Officer Siva replied. "The reason Fidel wants to leave is because—"

Officer Siva lowered his voice and looked

around cautiously. We all leaned in closer to listen. Even Watson.

"The real reason is because Luis, Fidel's son, has been receiving threatening letters," Officer Siva whispered.

"Threatening letters? Are they sinister?" I asked, my interest immediately piqued. "Who has been sending them?"

"We don't know yet. We don't even know if it's just a prank or something more serious," Officer Siva replied, still whispering.

"So Uncle Fidel approached you for help?" Wendy asked.

"Yes, but because we cannot tell if it's just a kid's prank or a real threat, the police cannot take official action. Fidel is quite worried," Officer Siva said. "Luis doesn't even know what's going on. He finds the letters in his school bag, but since all the letters are addressed to his dad, Luis has never read them. He doesn't know he's the target. He thinks it's part of some game called Chain Mail."

Chain Mail! That's the game that we've all been playing. Interesting.

"This is where we come in, isn't it, Officer Siva?" I said. "You would like us to investigate exactly who is sending sinister letters to Luis!"

"Does this mean you're taking the case, Sherlock?" Officer Siva said, grinning.

"It-is-known-that-Sherlock-will-investigate-for-food," Watson replied, as I ate more of my black carrot cake.

"Er, Sam, we should first ask Mom and Dad if it's okay," Wendy said.

"Don't worry, Wendy. I'll definitely check with your parents first," Officer Siva replied. "I just wanted to make sure Sherlock Sam and his Supper Club are on the case."

"Wait, why are we his Supper Club?" Wendy asked, wrinkling her nose. "I don't eat supper, and Sherlock isn't supposed to, either."

"I-would-like-an-explanation-as-well," Watson said. "He-only-ever-feeds-himself-and-not-just-supper."

I wanted to explain to Wendy what a supper club was, but I was too excited. Sinister letters! A threatened student! A new case! I couldn't wait to start! But first, I had to be thorough—

"By the way, Officer Siva, the international school has a big canteen, right?" I asked.

ooo

CHAPTER THREE

"What's that?" Jimmy said, pointing to a game being played on the basketball court. Four kids were bouncing a ball back and forth among them while they attempted to stay within four squares painted on the ground. We were standing at the playground of Enterprise International School, watching the kids play.

"I have no idea," Wendy replied.

"It looks like it's very popular," Nazhar said.

I observed the players carefully.

"The point of the game seems to be to get other players out of the game by bouncing the ball out of their square without them catching it," I said.

"Oh! Like Ping-Pong, but with a bigger ball and four players," Jimmy said. "And no table. Or paddles. And you're out after only one point. And the same person serves all the time until that person goes out . . ." Jimmy started counting all the differences with his fingers. He looked up helplessly at Wendy.

"So-not-really-like-Ping-Pong-at-all," Watson said.

"You guys have never heard of Four Square?"

We turned around and saw Eliza, but something was different about her. She was alone, without her group of friends who always followed her around, and she was toying with her braids, looking a bit nervous.

"What do you want, Eliza?" Wendy asked. "Why don't you go hang out with your friends and leave us alone?"

"I was just going to tell you about the game since you seemed so interested, but if you're going to be like that, forget it," Eliza said. She turned and stomped off, bumping into a startled Nazhar along the way.

"Maybe she's just lonely," Nazhar whispered. "All her friends are in other classes, so they didn't get to come for this exchange program."

"Nazhar, are you defending her?" Wendy asked. "She's a bully. If she's lonely, it serves her right for making fun of people."

Nazhar and I looked at each other and shrugged. Jimmy chased a butterfly that he had spotted in a nearby bush.

"Anyway, shouldn't we be looking for the classes we'll be attached to this week?" Wendy asked. "Sam, shouldn't you be making friends with that Luis kid?" Wendy didn't realize it, but she sounded a lot like Eliza when she was bossing us around. No one told her that, of course.

"Who's Luis?" Jimmy asked, giving up his butterfly chase.

I brought Nazhar and Jimmy up to speed on the mission Officer Siva had given us, word-for-word.

"Eh? How come we are your Supper Club?" Nazhar asked. "Also, what's a supper club?"

"I-have-yet-to-hear-an-explanation-I-can-accept," Watson said while Wendy nodded.

"You guys are focusing on the wrong thing," I said. "And anyway, it's not my Supper Club. We are all in the Supper Club together. It's like a superhero team! We're the Avengers!"

"I wanna be Superman!" Jimmy shouted. I couldn't bring myself to tell Jimmy that Superman wasn't an Avenger. He was so excited.

"Right, let's go find our classes," I said before anybody else could complain.

Jimmy and Watson followed me as we searched for our assigned class—Mrs. Chi's fourth grade class. All the elementary classes were lined up on the basketball court. Enterprise International School was smaller than our school, but it seemed to have a bigger playground and sports field. It had an elementary school, a junior high school, and a high school. The international school students wore a mix of light brown and dark blue uniforms. They did not seem to have a standard uniform. All the students from our school still wore our regular uniforms.

When the bell rang, a young and pretty Korean lady came to lead us up to our second-floor classroom. I deduced that she was Mrs. Chi. I could see the international school students looking at us curiously.

As we walked into the classroom, I looked at the wall of photographs and saw that this class had thirteen students: Alejandro, Elena,

Yae Lynn, Rachel, Joseph, Marissa, Nathan, Hana, Vineesha, Simon, Hannah, Tehillah, and the boy of the hour, Luis. Luis was Mexican, an ethnicity I admittedly knew very little about, and from the United States. The rest of the students seemed to come from all over the world!

Ten of my classmates huddled together at the back of the class. The rest of my classmates were in the other fourth grade classes. We were all feeling a bit shy—everyone but Jimmy, that is. He was bouncing around from wall to wall, exclaiming excitedly about the things that he saw. Reading lists! Letters to local businesses written by the kids! Class photographs! Arts and crafts!

Mrs. Chi formally introduced us to her fourth grade class. They said "Hi!" and waved cheerfully. Everyone seemed really friendly. Then we all shifted the tables and desks around to make room for my classmates and me. I made sure I ended up seated next to Luis. He grinned at me and offered me a mango pop that was covered in chili powder! I had never had a lollipop that was covered in chili powder before! I was already learning about something new. Jimmy sat next to Alejandro and they chatted away happily.

"We're going to start the reading aloud part of our lesson now. For the exchange kids, this is where we'll all read aloud from our chosen book and then we'll discuss what we've read, okay?" Mrs. Chi explained. "If anyone has a question, our rule is that you have to raise your hand and you can only speak if I point at you, understand?"

All of the international school students' hands immediately shot up. Mrs. Chi grinned and pointed at the girl to my left, Hannah.

"Why is there a robot at the back of the class?" Hannah asked. Everybody immediately turned to look at Watson, who was seated on the couch at the back of the room.

"Samuel, would you like to explain?" Mrs. Chi asked me. My regular teacher had called to explain about Watson. Watson couldn't participate in any of the lessons but he was given observer status.

"He's my robot," I said. "Would you like to introduce yourself?"

"My-name-is-Wat-son," Watson said. "I-am-not-allowed-to-discuss-my-secret-abilities."

Watson really didn't seem to understand the concept of "secret" abilities.

"And he's Sherlock! Sherlock Sam!" Jimmy said excitedly, pointing at me. All eyes in the classroom swung from Watson to me.

"Well, well, Sherlock and Watson, eh? Very interesting," Mrs. Chi said, her eyes sparkling. "Kids, you'll have more time to investigate Sherlock and Watson during lunch, okay? Now it's time for reading."

After the half-hour reading aloud session was over, Mrs. Chi took us to the school library to select one of five books to write book reports on. Apparently, the authors of these five books were going to be featured at the upcoming children's book festival in May. All the authors were either Singaporean or living in Singapore as permanent residents. When we reached the library, we immediately saw that Luis's dad, Fidel Alvarado, was one of the featured authors for his book *The Boy Who Thought He Could Fly*. Luis looked shy, but very proud. The four other books were *Why Peas Taste*

Green by Yvonne Zhang, *Wibbly Wobbly, Timey Wimey* by the Physician's Companion, *The Adventures of Trill the Robot and Sofa the Sofa* by Michael Yeo, and *Indestructible Shapes* by John Halson.

Right then, Wendy, Nazhar, Eliza, and a few of their fifth grade classmates came into the library as well.

I picked *Wibbly Wobbly, Timey Wimey* because it was a book about time travel; Jimmy picked *The Adventures of Trill the Robot and Sofa the Sofa* because he loved robots; Wendy picked *Why Peas Taste Green* because the author was known to write everything out by hand; and Nazhar picked *Indestructible Shapes* because he'd heard the author was kind of an eccentric fellow. Eliza picked Luis's dad's book. Based on what I knew about her, she did that because she liked knowing famous people.

"Watson, if you'd like to pick a book to write about, please go ahead," Mrs. Chi said.

Watson immediately selected *The Adventures of Trill the Robot and Sofa the Sofa.*

"What do you think happens now?" Jimmy whispered as he clutched his book.

"Children, listen up. We've done this project before, but I'm explaining it again for our exchange students. You will have two days to finish your books. Make sure you don't pick the same book as the first time," Mrs. Chi said. "Please write a letter to the author, asking him or her about his or her book. If your parents have given you permission, you may give the authors your home address, for them to write back to you. This is just like what you did for the first round of letters we wrote the last time. If not, use the school address. And make sure you ask intelligent questions!"

Mrs. Chi also explained that the school had arranged for us exchange students to get our response letters from the authors by Friday— our last day at Enterprise International School.

Just as Mrs. Chi finished, the lunch bell rang and all the kids cheered. We were instructed to put the books back in our respective classrooms before heading down for lunch.

"Now comes the important part," I said quietly. I was already thinking really hard.

"What's that, Sherlock?" Nazhar asked. The Supper Club had gathered around me.

"Deciding what to eat for lunch," I answered.

∞∞∞

CHAPTER FOUR

After a delicious meal of chicken fried chicken and a grilled cheese sandwich, we found Luis in line for the Four Square game. The line was quite long, so I couldn't talk to him right away. Luis finally got his turn to play, and worked his way up to the second square before he was taken out. When he finished, he saw us and walked over.

"Hey, guys. So how did that Sherlock and Watson thing happen?" Luis asked.

"What-do-you-mean?" Watson asked.

"Why are you guys called Sherlock and Watson?" Luis asked.

"Sherlock Holmes is one of my heroes, and I would like to be a great detective like him one day! Batman, too!" I said.

"So you named your robot Watson after Sherlock Holmes's partner?" Luis asked.

"No. I-was-named-by-Sherlock's-father," Watson said.

"Yeah, I was going to name him MEGA-DESTRO-TECHNO-BOT," I explained, "but my dad walked in at just the wrong time."

"I think it worked out better, Sam," Wendy said, nodding. I had to agree. Given Watson's personality, he was highly unlikely to mega-destroy anything or anyone.

"How about you? When did you and your family move to Singapore?" I asked. I needed to get information about the sinister letters without letting Luis know he was the target.

"We moved here a couple of years ago when I was eight," Luis said. "My mom, who's a kidney doctor, was offered a job here and she took it. My dad started writing only when he got here. It was hard for me to adjust to Singapore at first, but once I figured out my parents were staying for good, I had to accept that I wasn't going to see my friends back in California again. Now I have friends here, though, so it's okay."

I couldn't imagine leaving Jimmy and Nazhar, or any of my other friends, if my parents ever decided to move overseas. It would be really hard to leave!

"And . . . uh . . . have you gotten any letters recently?" Wendy asked as innocently as possible. She kept biting her nails, though, which, to me, looked like a giveaway.

"How did you know about that?" Luis asked, frowning suspiciously.

"Know about what?" I asked quickly. "Aren't you playing Chain Mail as well? Wendy and I received letters asking us to write about our favorite books."

A good detective needs to have a quick mind and always be ready to deal with the unexpected.

"I got one with a physics question," Nazhar said. "Can I show it to you later, Sherlock? It involved pi."

"Oh, right. I'd forgotten about that," Luis said, looking relieved. "I'm sorry I freaked out a little. Someone's been leaving letters for my dad in my bag, and every time I deliver a new letter, my dad looks scared. He tries to hide it, but I can tell."

"Do you know what the letters say?" Wendy asked immediately.

"No, they're sealed, and I don't want to open my dad's mail," Luis said. "But I also don't want to keep giving the letters to him."

"Do you know who they're from?" I asked. I already knew what Luis's answer would be but I wanted to make sure.

"No, they're just there when I get back from recess or lunch," Luis said. "I've never been able to catch who leaves them there."

"Why don't you hide somewhere and spy on your bag?" Jimmy asked.

"I've tried, but nobody ever comes when I hide in the classroom," Luis said. "The letters are really starting to freak me out."

"Sinister letters tend to have that effect on people—" I said.

"Why do you call them sinister letters?" Luis interrupted, looking shocked. "What do you mean? Are you saying they are threatening my dad or something?"

"The letters might just be a prank, Luis. It's nothing for you to be worried about yet. I promise," I said.

"Wait, I don't understand. How do you know anything about what's going on—" Luis said. But before he could continue, the bell rang to signal the end of recess.

"I promise I'll explain everything later," I said. "But now, we should get back to class."

Luis stared at me hard and finally nodded his head. I knew it would be difficult for him to be patient, under the circumstances. He ran off toward Mrs. Chi's classroom. PE was the next lesson.

I always keep my promises. I wasn't going to let anything happen to Luis. Officer Siva trusted me with this, and I wasn't going to let him or Luis down.

"Whoever is giving the letters to Luis must

be someone at this school, right, Sherlock?" Nazhar said.

"Not only that, I suspect it might be someone in his class," I said.

"Why do you say that, Sam?" Wendy asked.

"Because the culprit clearly knows when Luis is not at recess or lunch," I said.

"It can't be anybody in his class, Sherlock," Jimmy said. "I've talked to most of them, and they're super nice! Yae Lynn is from Korea, and Simon is from Germany, and his name is not pronounced SY-MON, it's pronounced SEE-MOAN. And Hana is Japanese, but Hannah is Australian. And Joseph is Korean-Chinese, but from the U.S., and Vineesha is Indian, but from England! They've come from all over the world!"

"Hmm, at least one of them isn't as nice as he or she is pretending to be," Nazhar said. "Or it could even be Mrs. Chi!"

"Tread carefully, Nazhar," I said. "We need

more information before we can definitely say anybody is doing anything. For all you know, it could be anyone who has access to the classroom and knows the class schedule. It may even be Luis himself, in a bid for attention."

"Oh, yeah, that's true," Nazhar said. "I didn't think about that."

"As-important-as-this-conversation-is-I-believe-we-need-to-get-ready-for-P-E," Watson said.

Jimmy, Watson, and I split off from Wendy and Nazhar, and went to class. Mrs. Chi dismissed us for PE and told us we could use the boys' restroom to change into our PE uniforms.

We rejoined our class on the field behind the elementary school building, where we found the tallest teacher I had ever seen in my life. He was so tall, I couldn't see his head properly!

"Hello, students. My name is Mr. Johnson, and this is my PE class," he said. "Before we play any sports, I need you all to limber up, so let's do some jumping jacks."

It didn't take a genius detective to figure out this was going to be my least favorite class. After the jumping jacks, Mr. Johnson had us run around the track. Jimmy sped around the track twice before I finally finished one lap.

"Okay, everybody, good job! Now, let's play some flag football!" Mr. Johnson shouted.

"Watson," I said. "Tell Mom she may have been right about my eating habits if I don't make it out of this alive."

I didn't even know what flag football was, but the name led me to believe that there would be a flag and a football involved, and most likely lots of chasing.

"I-think-a-better-use-of-my-time-would-be-to-record-you-attempting-to-play-flag-football," Watson said.

My robot needed a serious personality matrix upgrade.

ㅇㅇㅇ

CHAPTER FIVE

After the excruciating gladiatorial games that made up PE, the rest of the school day passed without much incident. We learned a bit of world history, and got some time to read the books we'd chosen earlier in the day.

After school, we walked out and saw Officer Siva waiting by the front gate.

"Hey, Supper Club!" he called out.

"What's that mean?" Eliza asked Nazhar. She seemed to appear out of nowhere. "And who's that?"

Nazhar looked surprised that Eliza was talking to him directly.

"He's Officer Siva," Nazhar said hesitantly. "He's a bit weird. He keeps calling us Sherlock's Supper Club."

"You know a policeman? Why did he give you guys a name?" Eliza asked bossily. "What did you do that you know policemen who give you names?"

"You remember those DVD bootleggers that got caught in Fort Canning Park?" Wendy asked. "That was us. We helped catch them. Try and make fun of that. C'mon, guys." She pulled Jimmy and me away from Eliza, but Eliza seemed to have Nazhar cornered.

"Hey, Officer Siva," I said. "We don't have much of a report to give you, unfortunately."

"That's not why I'm here, actually," he said. "I told Mr. and Mrs. Alvarado about you and how you were helping me out, and they want to meet all of you. They've invited you to dinner tonight!"

"Oh. I don't know if we can go," Wendy said. "We've got homework and Mom doesn't usually let us go out on school nights."

"Now, let's not be hasty," I said. "What kind of dinner are we talking about?"

Officer Siva chuckled. "I checked with your mom and dad already, and they were okay with it, but you can call them to make sure."

Wendy took Officer Siva's cell phone and called home.

"Okay, but seriously, what kind of dinner?" I asked.

"You'll have to wait to find out!" Officer Siva said, grinning.

Mom had indeed agreed to let us go for dinner, and Jimmy and Nazhar had been allowed to as well.

Nazhar was walking away from Eliza toward the car when Officer Siva said, "You can bring your other friend along, too."

"Oh, no, Officer Siva," Wendy started, "she's actually—"

"Thank you so much, Officer Siva," Eliza said in the sweetest voice I had ever heard from her. "Nazhar was just helping me catch up on the case, and I'd be ever so happy to help out."

"What's happening?" I asked Wendy in a whisper.

"She does this all the time at school," Wendy whispered back. "She's only nice when grown-ups are around."

"Of course you can help! I didn't realize you were part of the Supper Club," Officer Siva said.

"Actually, she's—" Wendy started.

"Thank you, Officer Siva!" Eliza said. As soon as Officer Siva turned around, she stuck her tongue out at Wendy.

Officer Siva waited for Luis to come out of the school. He greeted Officer Siva as "Uncle Siva" and was very surprised to see us all with him.

"I'm sure you've met them already, but let me re-introduce you to Sherlock Sam and the Supper Club! They helped me solve a case before, and now they're going to help me figure out what's going on with your dad."

"That's why you knew all about the letters!" Luis exclaimed. He suddenly grabbed me and gave me a big hug. "You're going to help my dad!"

"Yes, and trust me when I tell you that I will get to the bottom of this or my name isn't Sherlock—" I said.

"Your name isn't Sherlock, it's CHER LOCK," Wendy said. "So technically you would be CHER LOCK Sam."

She laughed so hard, she doubled over and gasped for air.

I glared at my sister.

"By the way, Luis, this is Wendy, my sister, and Nazhar, our friend. They're in Primary Five," I said.

Eliza cleared her throat.

"Oh, and this is Eliza," I said. "She's also in Primary Five."

"We should get something for Luis's parents," Wendy said. "They've invited us to their house for dinner, so it's only polite that we buy them a gift."

"Hey, Wendy, can I borrow two dollars?" I asked. "I want to get a hot dog."

"Sam, we're going to eat dinner in less than an hour!" Wendy said.

"But not at this moment, correct?" I asked.

Wendy gave me an incredulous look and walked away. I wasn't sure what had just happened. My logic had been flawless.

We bought some famously delicious pineapple tarts from L.E. Cafe on Middle Road and the nice auntie there gave us a box of scrumptious old-fashioned butter cupcakes for free! I munched on them as we walked to Luis's family's condominium on Niven Road.

Luis let us into the building and we took an elevator up. When we reached his floor, Luis raced to his front door and disappeared within. As the rest of us reached the door, a large man in an apron that said *Mariachi Jalisco* greeted us.

"*Bienvenidos a la Casa Alvarado!*" he said.

"That means 'Welcome to the Alvarado House,'" Officer Siva translated. "This is Mr. Fidel Alvarado."

"Hello, Uncle," we all said.

Uncle Fidel led us into his home. Delicious smells that were unfamiliar to me wafted over from the kitchen.

"Please, everybody, sit down and get ready for a feast!" Uncle Fidel said.

Jimmy and Watson sat on my right, and Officer Siva sat on my left, while Wendy, Eliza, Nazhar, and Luis sat across from us. The seats at the two ends of the table were for Uncle Fidel and Auntie Maria Olga, who were busy in the kitchen.

On the table, I saw dishes of shredded lettuce, diced tomatoes, chopped onions, sour cream, beans, shredded cheese, various sauces that I could only wonder about, and a flat bread of some kind in the center. It looked a lot like *prala*, but flatter.

Uncle Fidel brought in two plates full of shredded chicken and strips of beef. Auntie Maria Olga brought in a third plate full of something I had never seen before. It looked like large peppers fried in egg batter, but . . . was that for eating?

"By the looks on your faces, I can tell you've never had a meal like this before," Uncle Fidel said. "So let me explain: first, you take the tortilla"—he lifted the flat, *prata*-like bread from the middle of the table, and continued—"and put either chicken or beef in it. You can put both, but my wife will scold you, so I suggest sticking to one only."

He grinned as Auntie Maria Olga frowned at him.

"Then, put some beans on top, and fill up the tortilla with as many condiments as you like! There are fresh vegetables, tomato sauces, chiles, sour cream, and guacamole. The end result is a taco!" he said.

"What's guacamole, Uncle?" Wendy asked.

"It's mashed-up avocados with a little bit of lemon and tomato," Luis said. "It's super delicious on pretty much anything!"

"What-kind-of-beans-are-those?" Watson asked.

"These are pinto beans. They are a staple of Mexican cuisine, much like rice is a staple of Chinese cuisine. We put them on almost everything," Uncle Fidel replied.

"There-is-a-100-percent-chance-that-beans-will-make-Sherlock-fart," Watson said.

All the humans laughed. I glowered at Watson.

"And what are those?" Nazhar asked, pointing at the peppers.

"Those are *chiles rellenos*," Auntie Maria Olga said. "They're long peppers stuffed with cheese and fried in a flour-and-egg batter. They're kind of like the stuffed peppers you see at *yong tau foo* stalls, but these are a dish all by themselves."

I was intrigued, but also a bit worried. "Are they spicy, Auntie?"

"Well, some might be, but I cleaned out all the seeds, so the chances of you getting a spicy one are very small," she said.

"My mom makes the best *chiles rellenos* in the world!" Luis said.

"We also have some homemade *horchata*, which is a sweet rice drink with cinnamon," Uncle Fidel said.

"Oh! Like barley!" Nazhar said.

"Yes, but it's a different kind of sweet. I'm sure you guys will like it," Auntie Maria Olga said.

"Uncle Fidel, Auntie Maria Olga, you had me at 'feast,'" I said.

It was time to eat! Taking Uncle Fidel's suggestion, I piled up all the condiments in the tortilla, and had a rather messy first taco. But I learned quickly.

Over dinner, I asked Uncle Fidel about the Asian Children's Literature Prize. "You've won it the two years you've been living here, right, Uncle?"

"Yes, and the press conference for this year's award is at the end of this week," he said. "But I don't know if I'll win this year."

"Why not, *Papá*?" Luis asked.

"I haven't been able to write very well recently, and I might not finish my book," Uncle Fidel said. "Yvonne Zhang, who won second place the past two years, will probably win."

"I'm reading her book *Why Peas Taste Green*," Wendy said.

"I can relate to her disregard for peas," I said.

"That-is-good," Watson said. "Those-make-you-fart-too."

I was getting quite good at ignoring my robot.

"You'll win again this year, Uncle Fidel!" I said, confidently.

There was no way I would let the sinister letters get in the way!

ooo

CHAPTER SIX

Once the delicious dinner was over, it was time to focus.

"Uncle Fidel, would it be possible for me to inspect the sinister letters you have received?" I asked. We were standing a little away from the rest of the group.

"Of course, Sherlock. But perhaps we should do it in my study. I don't want Luis to get upset," he replied.

Auntie Maria Olga was holding an

impromptu Spanish class, and the Supper Club was failing miserably at rolling their *r*'s. Luis and Watson were trying to help them out. I motioned for Wendy to follow me because I knew that she had a skill that would be useful. She got up and walked over quietly.

Officer Siva, Wendy, and I stepped into Uncle Fidel's study and he walked over to his desk to pull out the letters from a locked drawer. While he was doing that, I took the time to observe my surroundings. He had wall-to-wall bookshelves filled with books! Dad and Mom would have loved to visit! Plus, he had one bookcase that was devoted to children's books! Luis was a lucky boy indeed.

"You have a lovely home, Uncle, and I'm sure you're doing everything possible to make Luis happy here, but is there any chance he is writing these letters himself?" I asked. "Maybe he's feeling homesick and wants to return to California?"

I didn't really think this was the case, but I had to look at every possible angle.

"When we first moved here, he took it pretty hard. He never believed we would stay for good. He considered this a vacation, even after Maria Olga told him her job was just too good to go back to the U.S. He was sure we would go back to California, back to his 'real school,' as he called it," Uncle Fidel said. "But now, this is his home. He hardly mentions California anymore, and when his mother or I broach the topic of visiting relatives there, he doesn't really want to go. No, I don't think this is him. He would talk to me if he had any problems."

I was convinced. There was no reason for Luis to act out in such a way. Uncle Fidel had put three envelopes on the table and was going to pull the letters out of them when I stopped him.

"Please wait, Uncle Fidel. The envelopes might have important clues as well," I said. "Right, Officer Siva?"

Officer Siva nodded.

"If the police were officially involved, we would run a fingerprint analysis. But this still cannot be classified as an official police case," Officer Siva said.

I picked up an envelope and looked it over carefully. There was no stamp, because the letter had been delivered by hand. It was a plain white envelope and looked to be of excellent quality. Why would the sender use such high-quality envelopes? I took the letter out. The paper was cream-colored and also looked to be of high quality. The words were written in capital letters:

MR. ALVARADO,
IF YOU DON'T STOP A'WRITING,
LUIS WILL GO A'MISSING.

"Is that supposed to be a short poem?" Wendy asked.

"If it is, it's a terrible one," I said. "Wendy, can you deduce any information from the handwriting?" The reason I had asked Wendy to join us in the study was because my sister is an artist and had recently developed an interest in fonts and handwriting. I thought she might be able to help.

"Hmm, well, it's in all capital letters so it's hard to tell. The writer is clearly trying to disguise his or her handwriting," Wendy replied.

She rubbed the sheet of paper between her fingers, and continued, "This is really nice paper."

"I noticed that as well," I said. "It's odd that someone would use such high-quality writing materials, don't you think?"

"That's a waste of money for sure," Officer Siva said.

"It's high-quality paper. I don't think you

can get this from just any stationery shop. Mom usually goes to the Bras Basah Complex when I need special paper for my art projects," Wendy said. "There are tons of art supply shops there. I've never been, though."

"That's the old multistory building near the National Library, isn't it?" I said. "Dad goes there to buy secondhand books. I've never been inside, either."

"Yep, we should go investigate," Wendy replied. "Maybe Mom will take us."

I thought that was a fantastic idea. I knew Wendy's knowledge of art and related things would be useful for this case!

"Can you tell if it's just one of Luis's classmates playing a nasty prank on him?" Uncle Fidel asked. He looked increasingly worried.

"I'm sorry. I can't tell if this was written by an adult or a child, Uncle Fidel," Wendy said, looking intently at the letter.

I pulled out the other two letters, and each one had a short, terrible poem as well:

MR. ALVARADO,
YOUR SCRIBBLIN' MUST STOP,
LEST YOUR BOY BE CAUGHT.

And:

MR. ALVARADO,
TAKE A BREAK FROM YOUR COMPOSITION,
OR LUIS WILL BE MISPOSITIONED.

All of a sudden, I noticed something. There seemed to be indentations on one of the letters. I quickly asked for a pencil and shaded lightly over the indentations. Faint words slowly started appearing.

"I suspect this might be the writer's true handwriting," I said, holding up the letter for everyone to see.

"That's very clever, Sherlock," Officer Siva said. "I have to admit I focused so much on what the sinister letters were saying that I completely missed this hidden clue."

The markings were written in cursive but were too faint for Wendy to make a proper analysis.

"I think it says: 'and they test fumbly' or 'and they tease bunny'?" Wendy read out. She was squinting really hard at the faint markings. "This is worse than the time I tried to read Jimmy's chicken scratches."

"'And they tease bunny'?" Uncle Fidel repeated. "What does that mean?"

"I don't know, but now we do know these letters are very specific. And very vague at the same time," I said. "This person, whoever it is, clearly wants you to stop writing for some reason, but he or she never openly states that Luis will be kidnapped. The person just hints at it."

"Then it must be an adult, correct?" Uncle Fidel asked. "Kids would be more obvious."

"Not necessarily. The person might not know that he or she is being vague. He or she is just trying to rhyme his or her terrible poems," I said. "And these poems are very amateurish."

"What would the motive be, Sam?" Wendy asked.

"Maybe this person doesn't want to do any more book reports?" I said. "It's a weak reason, I know, but never underestimate a kid's distaste of homework. Not me, of course, but other kids."

Uncle Fidel suddenly broke into rapid Spanish and walked around the room wringing his hands. He was so upset he had forgotten his English. Officer Siva stepped in front of him to try to calm him down.

"Don't worry, Uncle Fidel," I said. "Officer Siva put me on this case and I will not let him, you, Auntie Maria Olga, or Luis down. You can count on Sherlock Sam and the Supper Club!"

◦◦◦

CHAPTER SEVEN

"I thought we were here to investigate the case?" Wendy said, tapping her foot impatiently.

Dad and I looked up guiltily from the stack of books we had been browsing through at one of the many secondhand bookstores at the Bras Basah Complex.

Dad and Mom had picked us up from Enterprise International School after lessons on Tuesday, and we went to the shopping complex afterward. Nazhar and Jimmy had obtained permission to come along as well.

The building looked much older than most of the modern shopping centers in Singapore, and it housed many bookstores, art supplies and stationery shops, and shops that specialized in printing customized stationery. Mom said lots of students from nearby art schools like the Nanyang Academy of Fine Arts and LASALLE College of the Arts came here to buy art supplies.

Once we had told Dad and Mom we needed to find out more about the high-quality paper and envelopes the previous night, Dad immediately volunteered to take the day off and accompany us to the Bras Basah Complex. Mom then said she had better come along, too, so that Dad wouldn't buy too many books. The way I heard Mom explain it to Dad was, "Space is finite," which, of course, didn't make sense as the universe, and the space in it, is infinite.

"I guess we should head to one of the art supplies stores," I said, reluctantly putting the comic book I was holding down. "Come on, Watson."

Watson put the book on robotics that he was reading down, too. It just occurred to me that my robot might be capable of making his own upgrades. I would need to watch him carefully.

"We can come back later, Sam," Dad whispered to me.

I nodded. Solving the Case of the Sinister Letters was definitely more important. What was I thinking?

We took the escalator to the third floor. Wendy said there was a big specialized art supplies shop there, and that seemed the best place to start.

"Brrrrrras Basah is a funny name," Jimmy said, giggling to himself as he rode up the escalator. "Brrrrrrras Basah Brrrrrras Basah." He was trying to roll his *r*'s the way Auntie Maria Olga had taught him.

"Bras Basah actually comes from the Malay words *beras basah*, which mean 'wet rice,'" Nazhar said.

"Why did they name this place after wet rice?" Wendy asked. "That's a strange name for a place."

"Eh . . . from what my dad told me, it was because rotten wet rice used to be transported from sailing ships in the harbor through this area. It was really smelly," Nazhar said. "In fact, it was so smelly that the local papers wrote an article about it, called 'The Night Soil Carriers.'"

"Night soil? What are night soil carriers?" Wendy asked, wrinkling her nose. We had reached the third floor and were gathered in front of the art supplies shop.

"Nazhar, do you know what they are?" Dad asked. I had told him about Nazhar's interest in history. Nazhar's dad loved history the same way my dad loved science.

"My dad told me that as well," Nazhar replied. "Night soil carriers were people who collected human waste to throw away."

"Human . . . waste?" Wendy said, wrinkling her nose even more.

"You mean . . . POOP?!" Jimmy asked, wide-eyed.

"Yes, kids," Dad said. "This was way before the invention of the flush toilet, so people had to manually dispose of—"

"The toilet in my house has a seat that warms itself automatically when it gets cold," a familiar voice said from behind us.

We spun around.

"Eliza!" Wendy said in shock. "What are you doing here?"

My sister definitely didn't sound happy.

Eliza was in her school uniform, and she had come to the Bras Basah Complex with her family helper, the same helper that usually picked her up from school in a taxi.

"Hello, Auntie and Uncle, my name is Eliza. I go to school with Wendy and Sam!" Eliza said chirpily to my parents. Wendy was right; Eliza was very different in front of adults. Curious.

"I heard that Sherlock was coming here to investigate his latest case and I thought I could help!" Eliza said, smiling prettily.

"We don't need your—" Wendy said.

"Let's go in!" Eliza said, pulling Nazhar's

arm. He turned and gave us a helpless look as he stumbled after her.

"So that's Eliza," Mom said.

"Yeah," Wendy replied unhappily.

"I see what you mean," Mom continued, patting Wendy on the shoulder. "Let's go in. Your brother has a case to solve and he could use our help."

Eliza had already cornered a shop assistant and motioned us over. I didn't like taking orders from her, but time was of the essence!

"Hello, Auntie," I said to the shop assistant. I took the envelope and letter that I had borrowed from Uncle Fidel out of my backpack. "Do you know if this envelope and paper are readily available here?"

The shop auntie took both items from me and examined them closely.

"Yeah, yeah, we have. We have many different kinds of paper. You want to buy for your art project? This one is too expensive.

I recommend you cheaper one. Don't waste money!" the shop auntie replied.

"It's okay," I said, taking the envelope and the paper back from her. "Are you the only shop that sells this sort of envelope and paper?"

"No, *lah*, many of the shops here sell. But our shop has the biggest range of different kinds of paper. And if you buy in bulk, we surely give discount!" the shop auntie replied.

Wendy ended up buying some special art paper and paint, and we left the store soon after.

"Well, that was totally pointless," Eliza said.

"No one asked you to come," Wendy replied.

Mom shook her head at Wendy. Our parents always said that even if someone was mean, we should still try to be nice. Wendy looked at her shoes and didn't say anything after that.

"That's not entirely true, Eliza," I said. "At least we now know not to chase this particular lead any further. That will allow us to focus on other clues."

Eliza shrugged and fiddled sulkily with her pigtails.

"Eliza, do you need us to give you a ride home, too?" Dad asked.

"No need, Uncle, thank you," Eliza said sweetly, her attitude changing immediately. She and her helper left to look for a taxi to go home.

"What's next, Sherlock?" Nazhar asked.

"Since this was a dead end, we'll need to take a more direct route to solving the mystery," I said. "It might be riskier, but time is of the essence!"

"What does that mean?" Jimmy asked. "Like chicken essence?"

"We are going to catch the culprit in the act!" I replied.

ooo

CHAPTER EIGHT

"I-am-not-foliage," Watson said.

It was Wednesday, and we were back in school. I was trying to convince Watson that he needed to remain in the classroom during lunch and use his new holographic recording ability in case the culprit decided to put letters in Luis's bag!

"I know you're not a plant, Watson, but I'm asking you to pretend to be one, or at least hide behind that fern over there so that we can catch this guy," I said.

I really needed to install a camouflage function in Watson. Then he would be able to change colors and even pretend to be a giant hamburger!

"Please, Watson?" Luis said. "You're our only hope."

"I-will-do-this-only-because-Luis-asked-me-nicely," Watson replied, looking at me.

With Watson safely hidden behind the giant fern in Luis's classroom, the rest of us went down to the canteen for lunch. I had a delicious chicken wing and a slice of pizza.

"Wow, Sherlock. You really like to eat!" Luis said. "You could be Mexican!"

Wendy laughed so hard she almost fell off the bench. Even Nazhar couldn't hide his smile.

Just then, the bell rang, signaling the end of lunch. We were all anxious to view Watson's recording, but it was time for language arts and that meant that we had to write letters to the authors whose books we had selected. The recording would have to wait until recess.

I wrote a letter to the author of *Wibbly Wobbly, Timey Wimey* politely asking about the inconsistencies in the science and maths relating to time travel in the book. I also congratulated the author on picking a very clever pseudonym—the Physician's Companion. I recognized a *Doctor Who* fan when I encountered one.

I peeked over at Luis and saw that he was writing a letter to the author of *Indestructible Shapes*, John Halson, asking him what his favorite shape was. Jimmy looked up at me and waved his sheet of paper about. He had drawn lots of robots that looked suspiciously like Watson.

Once everyone was done writing their letters, Mrs. Chi gave us envelopes to put our letters in and collected them all. I checked the clock in the classroom and saw that we still had an hour until recess! I knew Luis and Jimmy were just as anxious as I was to view Watson's recording. Fortunately for all of us, the hour passed quickly and the bell signaling recess soon rang.

Jimmy, Luis, Watson, and I made our way down to the corner of the basketball court. That was our prearranged meeting place, and Wendy and Nazhar soon joined us.

"Let the meeting of Sherlock Sam and his Supper Club begin!" Jimmy said.

"We-are-not-his-Supper-Club," Watson said.

"Supper clubs are things grown-ups do. You all are just kids," a voice said from behind us.

We turned around.

"Eliza!" Wendy said. My sister didn't look at all happy to see her classmate. "Please stop eavesdropping."

I didn't like Eliza any more than Wendy did, but I had noticed Eliza sitting by herself during lunch and recess the past two days. It was likely that she didn't have any friends to eat with, and that was a very sad thing. Plus, if we were nice to her, maybe she'd be nice to us.

"It's okay, Wendy," I whispered to my sister. "You're here to protect us from her. What can she do? Besides, we don't have much time." She nodded but still didn't look happy.

I pushed the button on Watson's tummy and a beam of light shot out.

"Whoa!" Jimmy said.

We all watched as absolutely nothing happened for five minutes.

"This is boring," Eliza said.

Right at that moment, the recording showed the classroom door opening and someone stepping in. Luis gripped my arm. His face was pale and he looked terrified. It was Alejandro! He closed the door securely, went over to Luis's bag, and put a letter in it! Alejandro was the culprit!

"But he's so nice!" Jimmy said. "He can't be the bad guy!"

"Hey! That's awesome! Watson is just like R2-D2!" another voice said from behind us.

We spun around.

It was Alejandro! In the flesh!

We all looked at one another and simultaneously decided on the same course of action.

We gave chase!

Alejandro gave a loud yelp, threw the basketball he was holding, and dashed away.

We chased him through the football field, where Nazhar got hit in the stomach by a stray football. Alejandro ran to the playground and under the slide. Jimmy followed, but was caught by Rachel and Nathan, who started a tickle attack. Jimmy was lost! He would never escape from the dreaded tickle monsters! Luis

had almost caught up with Alejandro when he stumbled on the grass. Meanwhile, Wendy got tangled up in a basketball game on the nearby courts.

Alejandro kept going, past the playground and through the canteen, where I finally had to stop. I was made for thinking, not running. Then, Eliza was the last one left. She finally caught Alejandro as he tried to lose her in the classrooms. Wendy joined them as Eliza brought him back to the canteen. He looked extremely confused, so I guessed he didn't want to mess with the two girls.

"Really, Sam? This is where your legs gave out?" Wendy asked as they walked over to where I was.

"I do not control when my body gets tired," I said, munching on a hamburger.

I turned my attention to Alejandro. "Why are you putting letters in Luis's bag?" I questioned in between burger bites.

He looked confused. "What are you talking about?"

"You put a letter in Luis's bag during lunch. Don't deny it," Wendy said.

"Yeah, why did you do it, Alejandro?" said Luis angrily. He and Nazhar had finally caught up to us. "What did my dad ever do to you?!"

"What? Do what to whom? Yeah, of course I put the letter in there. Why would I deny it?"

Alejandro asked. "It's part of the game."

"What game?" Nazhar asked.

"The Chain Mail game?" Eliza said. "The one that everyone's playing?"

"Yeah," Alejandro said. "I've been getting letters with instructions to put other letters inside Luis's bag. The game is ruined now that he knows it's me."

"If you're just playing a game, then why did you run?" Eliza asked.

"I'm from New York, man! My dad told me: When someone chases you, you run!" Alejandro said.

Luis thought about it for a bit and said, "Like in L.A."

Alejandro and Luis grinned at each other.

"Can we take a look at these letters with the instructions you received?" I asked.

"They're at home, but I can bring them for you tomorrow," Alejandro said.

"That would be great, thanks," I said. We

would have to wait until tomorrow to discover if those instructions had any clues. And I would have to ask for permission before opening this latest sinister letter. I did not like waiting! Not when there was a mystery to be solved!

Alejandro went off to play basketball with Elena, Marissa, and Tehillah. Nazhar had already joined us at the table, but Jimmy was still being tickled at the playground. Watson decided to finally join us.

"And where were you while we were running ourselves ragged?" I asked Watson.

"I-was-comparing-the-fern-in-Mrs.-Chi's-classroom-with-the-bush-in-the-basketball-court. They-are-both-very-interesting-plants."

"Oh, *now* plants are interesting," I muttered under my breath.

"So, you guys solve mysteries all the time?" Eliza asked. "That's . . . that's actually kind of cool."

"You're only saying that because you have no one else to hang out with," Wendy retorted.

"No, I'm not. I really think it's cool," Eliza said. "But you guys are still nerds."

"That's a bit better, I guess," Nazhar said, shrugging his shoulders.

Jimmy suddenly ran up, out of breath. "What did I miss?" He grinned his enormous Jimmy grin.

ᴏ ᴏ ᴏ

CHAPTER NINE

"Why do these have crayon marks all over them?" Jimmy asked the next day.

Jimmy was looking at the original envelopes that were addressed to Alejandro. They had contained both the instructions for Alejandro to put the envelopes addressed to Uncle Fidel in Luis's bag and those envelopes themselves. We were in the canteen during lunch. The original envelopes that Alejandro had received were covered in colorful crayon markings.

"Oh, I have a little brother and he's just learning to draw," Alejandro replied, shrugging his shoulders.

"When Sam was three, he used to write equations in crayon on our walls," Wendy said. "It drove Mom crazy when Dad told Sam that he did a good job."

What Mom didn't know was that Dad was the one who had started writing in crayon on the walls first. It was his way of teaching me equations. He just forgot to use washable crayons.

"So, Alejandro, can you explain exactly what your letters have been instructing you to do?" I said.

"Okay. See? It says that in order to stay in the Chain Mail game, I will have to take this letter that's addressed to Fidel Alvarado and put it in his son's bag, when Luis isn't around," Alejandro said as he showed us the latest letter he received. "Sorry, man. If I had known what these letters were, I would never have done it."

Luis waved his hand to show that it was okay, but he still looked worried and tense.

Alejandro's letters were also written in very precise capital letters, just like Uncle Fidel's letters. It was almost as if someone had used a ruler to form all the letters. Someone was taking a lot of care to keep his or her identity a secret. The letters to Alejandro were far longer than the letters to Luis's dad. And like Uncle Fidel's letters, the paper used was of very good quality.

"And you didn't think the instructions were weird at all?" Eliza asked. She and Wendy rolled their eyes and exchanged an incredulous look. Wendy might not admit it, but I think she rather enjoyed having another girl around.

Alejandro went to play basketball, but he left all the letters for us to look through.

"I called Uncle Fidel last night and he gave me permission to open the latest sinister letter," I said. "Luis, are you ready for this? Your dad said he explained to you last night what's been going on."

Luis nodded, his arms folded tightly across his chest. I opened the envelope carefully.

MR. ALVARADO,
YOUR STORY BEST BE UNDONE,
LEST UNTOWARD BEFALL YOUR SON.

"Wow, that's really awful," Luis said. "No wonder Officer Siva thought it was a school prank. Would an adult really write this horribly?"

Luis seemed less afraid after seeing how terribly written the supposedly threatening letter was.

"He or she used *untoward* incorrectly," Wendy said, wrinkling her nose.

"How did this person get Alejandro's address?" Nazhar asked. "Children's names aren't listed in the telephone directory."

"I was just thinking the same thing, Nazhar," I said. "How indeed."

I shelved this question away so that I could think about it more carefully later. I felt it in my bones that this was a very important clue.

"We could go to the post office to ask the post office auntie where the letter came from!" Jimmy said.

"Unfortunately not, Jimmy. The letter

doesn't have a return address. I don't think the post office would be able to tell us where this letter was dropped off," I said.

I picked up the original envelopes that Alejandro had received to investigate if there were any clues left behind. So far, we'd only seen the envelopes that were addressed to Luis's father. Upon investigation, I discovered that both sets of envelopes were of the same high-quality paper.

I also noticed that the stamps were Singapore stamps, so we knew for a fact that the letters were being mailed locally.

I then brought one of the envelopes close to my nose to take a sniff. It smelled like cheese, but that was most likely from the cheese sandwiches Mom had made me for breakfast.

Just then, I spotted something underneath the crayon markings.

"Take a look at the stain on this envelope, everyone," I said.

"That's just crayon, Sherlock!" Jimmy said.
"It's not important!"

Not important? Unlikely!

"Wendy, does this look like fountain pen ink to you?" I said. Dad was a huge fountain pen fan and was constantly staining his shirts and fingers.

"Let me see," Wendy said as she took the envelope and used her fingernail to scratch away the crayon markings. "It does. It looks like . . . purple fountain pen ink!"

"Watson, please find out if Alejandro's family uses fountain pens," I instructed.

"This-is-why-I-am-such-a-slender-robot," Watson said as he walked slowly toward where Alejandro was playing basketball with his friends.

"Why didn't you do that yourself, Sherlock?" Eliza asked. "It would have been much faster, wouldn't it?"

"I forgot that Watson didn't have wheels installed so that he could speedily make his way over there," I said. I really needed to install all those upgrades I'd been planning for my robot.

"Alejandro-said-his-family-does-not-use-fountain-pens," Watson said when he returned a million seconds later.

"So it's possible that this stain was made by the person who sent the threatening letters," Eliza said.

"Yes, it's possible, but it's still not conclusive," I said. "It could have been made by a careless postal worker as well. Still, it's a clue that we should keep in mind."

"It honestly seems like there are no clues at all," Eliza said. "I thought this would have been more exciting."

She was right. It did seem that way. But I knew that all of this information fit together somehow. Solving a mystery was like putting a puzzle together, only you didn't know how many pieces there were in total, and there were no corner or border pieces to help guide you, either. But there is always one key piece. By itself, it's almost meaningless, but it ties every other piece together to give you a complete picture.

We were still missing that key piece.

ooo

CHAPTER TEN

"Can you belicve this?" I asked Eliza.

It was our last day at Enterprise International School, and we were looking through the replies we had received from the authors we had written to. The Physician's Companion wrote that she was happy there were young fans of *Doctor Who*, and that I should not be too concerned about the science in science fiction books, as the story was more important than getting the science and maths exactly right.

"A science fiction story does not work if it doesn't have a proper foundation of science to work from!" I said. "It's perfectly okay to invent your own technology, but it needs to have a proper scientific base. You can't just say a laser cannon shoots a million joules of energy. What creates that energy? Where does it come from? The law of conservation of energy clearly states energy can't be created out of thin air!"

Eliza stared at me blankly.

"You'll get used to these sudden outbursts. He calms back down when he realizes no one has any idea what he's talking about," Wendy said.

"What does your letter say?" I asked Eliza, ignoring Wendy.

"Luis's dad said that as long as I keep reading, he'll keep writing," Eliza said. "And that it was nice to meet me the other day."

"I think Mr. Halson wrote me back in code," Nazhar said. "I don't understand a word of this."

"Ooooh! A code! We'll crack it later!" I said.

"Mr. Yeo said that my robots are super cool, and that he might use some of them in his next Trill and Sofa book!" Jimmy said.

"He-asked-me-to-pose-for-his-next-book," Watson said. "I-am-going-to-be-a-supermodel."

"What about you, Wendy?" Eliza asked.

"Ms. Zhang said that I should always try to be the best, no matter what," Wendy replied.

"Remember, everyone, we're going to my place after school to go over all our clues," I said.

We enjoyed our last day fully. We finally got a chance to play Four Square at recess (we were terrible at it) and we had a party with delicious pineapple upside-down cake to celebrate our last day. It was amazing: it had pineapple and it was upside down!

I was going to miss our new friends, but not as much as Jimmy was going to. They put up one of his robot drawings on the wall, as well as the drawing he made of Mrs. Chi's fourth grade class. I talked to Luis again and assured him that I would get to the bottom of the Case of the Sinister Letters no matter what!

After school, Eliza, Nazhar, and Jimmy followed Wendy, Watson, and me home.

"Okay, let's go over all our clues," I said.

"If we can even call them that," Eliza said.

"The letters are addressed to Uncle Fidel,

and they tell him to stop writing his book," Wendy said, frowning at Eliza.

"And while Uncle Fidel is clearly meant to think something will happen to Luis if he doesn't stop writing, it's never made clear what," Nazhar said. "Almost as if the letter writer knows the police cannot get involved if he is vague."

"The letters are written as poems," Jimmy said.

"Terrible-rhyming-couplets," Watson added.

"The letters were originally sent to Alejandro to give to Luis to pass to his dad," Wendy said. "The letter writer knows where Alejandro lives but not where Uncle Fidel lives."

"No, he is clearly trying to cover his tracks by not sending the letters directly to Uncle Fidel," I said.

"Why do you say that, Sherlock?" Nazhar asked.

"Whoever this person is clearly knows Uncle Fidel well enough to know he's writing a book and where his son goes to school. It is reasonable to assume that this same person might know where they live as well," I said.

"We also have all the letters sent to Uncle Fidel, as well as the letters sent to Alejandro, and they all have the same carefully constructed handwriting, so that no handwriting analysis can be made," Eliza said. "I wonder why the person didn't just type it out on a computer and print it out?"

"That's something that has been puzzling me as well," I said. "It would have been easier to just let a computer mask the handwriting instead of going to all this trouble. Why bother?"

There seemed to be more questions than answers. It was extremely frustrating but challenging at the same time!

"And finally, we have this pencil rubbing of what we think the letter writer's actual handwriting looks like," Wendy said. "I still think it says 'and they tease bunny,' which I know doesn't help us at all."

"Maybe it's aliens who broke the space-time continuum," Wendy said finally.

Everyone stared at her.

"What? Sam's the only one who can talk about aliens?" Wendy replied.

"That's ridiculous," I said. "You cannot break the space-time continuum. You can, however, bend it. But we have seen no evidence of any of this, Wendy. Don't be silly."

"How come when you and Dad talk about it, it's not silly?" Wendy said.

"Because when we talk about it, it's based on SCIENCE!" I said, striking the pose that Dad and I usually made when we said "SCIENCE!"

"I think these clues might all be dead ends, Sherlock," Nazhar said.

"I don't think that's true, Nazhar," I said. "I just need some time to put everything together."

"He-needs-Milo-and-double-chocolate-Khong-Guan-biscuits-to-think," Watson added.

Eliza, Nazhar, and Jimmy went home, and I stared at the letters for a long time. I knew I was missing a piece of the puzzle, but I didn't know what that piece was.

"Hey, Sam, I almost forgot. We got a letter from Uncle Fidel," Wendy said, digging into her bag and pulling out a letter. "He's inviting us to the Asian Children's Literature Prize press conference tomorrow at the National

Library. I think Nazhar, Jimmy, and Eliza received invites, too."

She handed me a letter and I looked through it. "I think you gave me the wrong letter, Wendy. This isn't from Uncle Fidel, it's from — "

I stared at the letter. I couldn't believe it.

"Does this look familiar to you?" I asked Wendy, showing her the letter.

Wendy squinted at the letter for a while.

"It does," Wendy replied. Her eyes widened. "Do you think . . . ?"

"I do," I said.

We were definitely going to the press conference, and I was going to prove who had been sending sinister letters to Uncle Fidel!

ooo

CHAPTER ELEVEN

"You're wearing THIS to the press conference?" Wendy asked incredulously.

"Yeah! Dad helped me pick my outfit! Nice, right?" I said, straightening out my green polka dot bow tie and pressing down my blue shirt and brown checkered pants neatly.

"Has Mom seen you?" Wendy continued.

"Yeah, she did. She asked if Dad helped me pick my outfit. Why?" I said.

"Never mind," Wendy said, shaking her

head. "At least Watson looks good."

"I-always-look-good," Watson replied. He had on a tuxedo with a black bow tie. I thought it was too plain.

We arrived at the Asian Children's Literature Prize press conference. It was held at the Pod at the top of the National Library on Victoria Street, and there were already tons of people there. Some of them were even famous!

"Look, there's Nazhar, Eliza, and Jimmy,"

I said, pointing and waving. They were all formally dressed as well. Jimmy was wearing his dinosaur *batik* shirt!

"Excellent. Now we just need to wait for Uncle Fidel and Luis." Just as I said that, I spotted the Alvarado family. Auntie Maria Olga was wearing a nice black dress, while Uncle Fidel looked distinguished and elegant in a handsome gray suit. However, instead of looking relaxed, he looked tense. I also noticed that he kept a firm hold on Luis's shoulder and wouldn't let his son stray far away from him. He wouldn't have to worry about Luis's safety for much longer!

Officer Siva was there as well, probably also invited by Uncle Fidel. Even though he was there in an unofficial capacity, he still wore his police dress uniform.

I wandered through the thick crowd, trying to find the person responsible for all this. After a few minutes and much polite excusing, I found her. Even from a distance I could see that the shirt she was wearing had a dark purple ink stain on the front pocket. I recognized stains like that because Dad had them all the time when his fountain pen leaked into his pocket. It was a dark purple stain that matched the purple ink stain on the envelope that Alejandro had received from the letter writer!

I stepped in front of her and stuck my hand out. Wendy was by my side and had signaled the rest of the Supper Club to join us.

"Oh! Hello there, little boy. Aren't you cute," Yvonne Zhang said as she reached out to shake my hand. Instead of wearing an evening dress, like most of the women at the press conference, she was clad rather casually in an Oxford men's shirt and black slacks. The purple ink stain was even more prominent up close.

"I'm really glad to meet you, Ms. Zhang," I said. "My sister, Wendy, and I are big fans of your new book, *Why Peas Taste Green*."

Out of the corner of my eye, I saw Nazhar politely request that Uncle Fidel, Auntie Maria Olga, and Luis join us as well.

"Oh, how wonderful," Ms. Zhang said. "I love meeting my young fans. Do you want me to autograph your copy? You did buy one, right?"

"Is it true that unlike other authors, you write your stories on paper, using a pen?" I asked, evading her questions.

"That's true. I dislike modern technology. I still use a pen and paper for everything," she said. "All these other authors are always using the Internet for research and word processing programs to write. They can't even spell properly anymore! I don't have a computer at home, and I refuse to get one of those terrible smartphones that keep you connected all the time."

"You must spend a lot of money on paper," I said.

"Yes, I only use high-quality paper," Ms. Zhang replied. "If not, the ink from my fountain pen would soak through."

By this time, Nazhar, Eliza, Jimmy, Watson, and the Alvarados had gathered around Wendy and me.

"Oh. Hello, Fidel," Ms. Zhang said frostily. "I didn't expect you to attend. I heard that you're having problems with your next book. You might want to consider spending more time at home writing it rather than attending press conferences, perhaps?"

"And perhaps you might want to try working harder at your horrible poetry!" I said as I pointed a finger at Ms. Zhang accusingly.

"Sherlock! What are you doing?" Uncle Fidel asked, looking shocked.

"She's the one who has been sending you sinister letters, Uncle Fidel!" I said.

"What a terrible thing to accuse me of, little boy," Ms. Zhang said. "What proof do you have? I could sue!" Her eyes had narrowed and her fists were clenched tightly at her sides. A bunch of reporters showed up out of nowhere.

"Well, for one thing, you have Alejandro's home address," I said.

"Alejandro? The boy from that international school who wrote about my book for his book report a few weeks ago? So what?" Ms. Zhang said.

"It isn't easy to find out a kid's home address, especially with the precautions that his parents and the Enterprise International School have taken," I said. "The only way you would have his address is if he gave it to you after receiving permission from his parents."

"He did. But the only time I wrote to him was to thank him for his nice letter," Ms. Zhang insisted. "That proves nothing!"

"It proves that you had his address!" I said. "And when you sent the sinister letters through him, you made him think it was part of the Chain Mail game!"

Ms. Zhang sputtered in anger.

"One of the things that I couldn't figure out, which Eliza pointed out, was why someone would bother to disguise his or her handwriting. Wouldn't it be easier to just use a computer and print the sinister letters out?" I said.

"The person used a ruler to painstakingly write out each letter," Wendy said. "It took a very long time."

"Ms. Zhang, you just said you hate technology, and that you don't even have a computer at home," Eliza said.

"Many people don't have computers at home," Ms. Zhang said. "I'm not going to stand here and be accused of this nonsense. Fidel, you should be ashamed of yourself, getting kids to do your dirty work!"

"Stop blaming my dad!" Luis yelled loudly. "You're a bad, bad person!"

Startled, the crowd in the room suddenly fell silent. All eyes were now on us.

It was time for my grand reveal.

"Wendy, if you don't mind," I asked my sister.

Wendy handed me the two sheets of paper.

"Do you recognize this letter, Ms. Zhang?" I asked, showing her the letter.

"It's . . . it's the letter I wrote in response to a child writing to me about how much she loved my new book," Ms. Zhang said nervously. "Where did you get it?"

"You wrote it to me!" Wendy said angrily.

"You're very competitive, even in this letter. 'Be the best, no matter what.' Even if 'no matter what' means threatening your competitors' children!"

"And do you recognize this, Ms. Zhang?" I asked again, holding up the letter with the pencil rubbing.

"I most certainly do not," Ms. Zhang said.

"Uncle Fidel, if you look closely at both of these sheets of paper, you'll realize something very obvious," I said, handing Uncle Fidel the two sheets of paper.

He took them both and stared closely at them.

"The handwriting is the same! And the paper is the same kind of high-quality paper!" Uncle Fidel yelled out. He passed the two sheets of paper to Auntie Maria Olga, who gasped in shock.

"We couldn't figure out what the pencil rubbing said at first. Wendy thought it said, 'and they test fumbly' or 'and they tease bunny,' didn't you, Wendy?" I asked my sister.

Wendy nodded vigorously; she was still glaring at Ms. Zhang.

"But what it actually said was 'and they taste funny'—a line from *Why Peas Taste Green*!" I said triumphantly. "You must have accidentally used a piece of paper that had been underneath another sheet of paper that you had used to write your story. You pressed so hard that you left an indentation on the lower sheet."

"Yvonne, how could you do something so terrible?" Uncle Fidel said.

By this time, a huge crowd had gathered around us and they were all muttering and shaking their heads in disbelief.

"It's your own fault!' Ms. Zhang said. "I was the bestselling children's author until you moved here two years ago with your family. I wasn't really going to do anything to your son, but I thought if you were worried enough about him, you wouldn't be able to finish your book in time to submit it for the Asian Children's Literature Prize next month!"

"And you thought if you could win that award, you would regain your popularity, didn't you?" I said.

"Yes! And I would have gotten away with it, too, if not for you *kaypoh* kids!" Ms. Zhang shouted.

"Ms. Zhang, I think perhaps you should come with me," Officer Siva said.

He carefully took hold of Ms. Zhang's arm and led her away.

"You can't do anything to me! I haven't done anything illegal!" Ms. Zhang shouted furiously, attracting even more attention.

Most of the reporters followed Officer Siva and Ms. Zhang out of the Pod.

"Wow, Sherlock, you really are a fantastic detective," Uncle Fidel said.

"Ready, Watson?" Jimmy asked.

"I-am-ready," Watson said.

"He's Singapore's Greatest Kid Detective!" Jimmy shouted.

"Only-when-he-does-not-have-to-play-sports," Watson said.

A photographer took a picture of Jimmy and Watson as I cringed behind Uncle Fidel.

ooo

About two months later, after Uncle Fidel's new book, *How to Build a Spaceship with Your Son*, was published, Mom came into my room while I was testing camouflage patterns on Watson.

"Did you see the papers today, Sam?" she asked.

She showed me the newspaper, and I read that Uncle Fidel had been awarded the Asian Children's Literature Prize.

"Good for him. He deserves it," I said. We still kept in touch with Luis and all the kids at

Enterprise International School.

"Did you read the part at the bottom?" she asked.

I read: "Yvonne Zhang was disqualified from the award. She moved to Australia, and has stopped writing children's literature after it was revealed that she had sent sinister letters through Mr. Alvarado's son, as discovered by Singapore's very own kid detective, Sherlock Sam."

"It's no big deal," I said. "I only did it to help Officer Siva and Uncle Fidel's family."

"And because the mystery needed to be solved," Mom said, kissing my forehead. "I'll cut this out, frame it, and put it with the other clippings in the living room."

"Speaking of needing to solve mysteries, there's something I've been meaning to ask you," I said, just as Mom was leaving.

"What did you and Dad do now?" she asked, turning around to look at me.

"Watson, please play the recordings," I said.

Since that first night Watson had caught Mom taking some Khong Guan biscuits after dinner, I had him check every night to see how often Mom got herself a late-night snack. She was in the kitchen pretty much every night, and Watson was playing all of the recordings.

"Sam! I—have you told Dad?" Mom asked. She looked shocked.

"Of course not, Mom!" I said. "This can be our secret."

I grinned at Mom and stuck out my little finger for a pinkie swear. Mom hooked her little finger through mine and we shook.

"It's just . . . by the time I've finished cooking, I'm too tired to eat, and I get hungry later in the evening," Mom said.

"I know, Mom. And I also know your favorite biscuit is the lemon cream," I said, still grinning.

Mom grinned back.

"I guess my son really is Singapore's Greatest Kid Detective," Mom said.

"Only because he has the best mom in the entire world," I replied.

GLOSSARY

Ang Moh—A Hokkien term that literally means "red hair." In this book, it is used affectionately to refer to Caucasians or Western culture in general.

Avengers—A superhero team published by Marvel Comics. Its members include Captain America, Iron Man, Thor, Hawkeye, Black Widow, and many others. Superman is NOT a part of the Avengers.

Batik—Traditional Javanese design made from dyeing cloth. This cloth is often used by Peranakans for shirts and sarongs.

Biscuit—Cookie.

Black Carrot Cake—There is no carrot in this carrot cake! In fact, this very popular Singaporean dish is not a dessert at all, but a savory dish of fried white radish and egg that can be eaten for breakfast, as part of a meal, or as a snack. Black carrot cake got its misleading name in translation, as the Chinese word for radish can also mean carrot.

Bras Basah Complex—A shopping complex in the heart of the Bras Basah–Bugis neighborhood in Singapore and next to the National Library. It was built in the 1980s and has been nicknamed the City of Books.

Chiles Rellenos—A Mexican dish that literally means "stuffed pepper." It originated in the city of Puebla and consists of a roasted, fresh, usually mild pepper stuffed with melted cheese and covered in an egg batter. It is usually served in a tomato sauce with a side of Mexican rice and refried pinto beans.

Doctor Who—The long-running British Broadcasting Corporation television series that features the Doctor, an alien Time Lord, and his human companions. The Doctor travels through time and space using his TARDIS, a British police box shaped time machine.

Durian— A southeast Asian tropical fruit that is known as the King of Fruits. It has a hard green spiky shell that houses a creamy yellow fruit with an impressively pungent odor. Not for the faint-hearted.

Durian Pengat—A traditional Peranakan dessert that is made of rich, warm, and sweet durian cream and pulp.

Hawker Center—A large food court (indoor or outdoor) where customers can buy a wide variety of foods from vendors (hawkers) at their stalls.

Horchata—A Mexican sweet drink made from rice, sugar, cinnamon, and sometimes vanilla.

Jalisco—A state in the central west part of Mexico. Many things typically associated with Mexico originated in Jalisco, including *mariachis*, the wide-brimmed *sombrero* hat, the Mexican hat dance, tequila, and rodeos called *charreadas* and *jaripeos*.

Junior High School—Many international schools in Singapore use the U.S.-style junior high school system, which consists of grades 7 and 8. This is the same as Secondary years 1 and 2 in Singapore schools.

Kaypoh—Nosy or meddling. A busybody.

Kopi—The Malay word for "coffee."

Kopitiam—The Malay word for "coffee shop," but in Singapore it often refers to a small collection of local eateries housed under the same roof.

Lah—Singaporean slang often used to end a sentence and to add emphasis. For example, "Cannot, *lah*!"

Law of Conservation of Energy—This law states that energy can be neither created nor destroyed, and therefore the sum of all the energies in a system is constant.

Mariachi—Folk music from Mexico. The term *mariachi* can refer to the music itself and the musicians and bands that play it. A traditional *mariachi* band has at least two violins, two trumpets, and one or more guitars, with members taking turns to sing.

Maths—Short for mathematics. In the United States and Canada, English speakers say "math," but in the United Kingdom (and some other places, like Singapore, which was once under British control), people tend to use the term "maths."

Pinto Beans—The most common bean in Mexico and the U.S. and a staple of Mexican cuisine. Very rarely do Mexican dishes not contain pinto beans, either whole or mashed and refried.

Prata—A fried Indian flat bread made of flour. Found all over Singapore, it can be ordered plain or filled with savory fillings (cheese, onion, egg, etc.) or sweet fillings (banana, cream, chocolate, etc.). It usually comes with a side of curry.

Primary Five—Fifth grade.

Rhyming Couplet—In poetry, these are two lines of the same length that rhyme and complete one thought. There is no limit to the length of the lines. This poetical device has been used by such renowned poets as William Shakespeare, Alexander Pope, John Dryden, Geoffrey Chaucer, and many others.

Supper Club—This is either a dining establishment that is also a social club, where people socialize while eating, or an underground restaurant that shows up only one night in a secret location known only to a few people. Officer Siva likely gave Sherlock Sam and his friends this name because he knows they like to eat and hang out while solving mysteries.

Wah—An exclamation used to express admiration.

Yong Tau Foo—A Chinese dish with Hakka origins, comprising fish balls and other items stuffed with minced meat or fish paste, including bitter gourd, eggplant, okra, peppers, and tofu. This dish can be eaten with or without soup.

ABOUT THE CHARACTERS

SAMUEL TAN CHER LOCK aka SHERLOCK SAM
Ten-year-old Sherlock Sam's heroes are Sherlock Holmes, Batman, and his dad. Extremely smart and observant, Sherlock loves solving any and all mysteries—big or small. He loves comics and superheroes!

WATSON
Built by Sherlock to be his trusty, cheery sidekick, Watson is, instead, a "grumpy old man" who is reluctantly drawn into Sherlock's adventures or, as Watson perceives them, his misadventures. Watson is environmentally friendly.

WENDY
Sherlock's older sister. A year older than Sherlock, Wendy is a very talented artist, but she is terrible at Chinese. Sherlock would like to be taller than her soon. She doesn't like wearing dresses or skirts.

JIMMY
Sherlock's classmate Jimmy is the only boy in a Peranakan family with four sisters. He seems much younger than his actual age because everything is exciting and magical to Jimmy. He has terrible handwriting.

DAD
An engineer, Sherlock's dad is a scientific genius, but is rather forgetful and bumbling in real life. He has never stopped reading superhero comics—a love he's passed on to his son.

MOM
A homemaker, Sherlock's mom is half-Peranakan and is constantly experimenting in the kitchen. Sherlock often wonders why she tempts him with food, then does not allow him to eat his fill.

NAZHAR
Usually shy and quiet, Nazhar will stand up for his friends when they are threatened. Sherlock admires him for his knowledge of history, which Nazhar learned from his dad. Nazhar believes in the supernatural, much to the dismay of Sherlock.

ELIZA
One of the prettiest and most popular girls in school, Eliza often bullies kids she sees as weird or geeky—for example, Sherlock Sam and his friends. Eliza spends a lot of time in front of the bathroom mirror, making sure her hair is neat.

OFFICER SIVA
A deputy superintendent in the Singapore Police Force, Officer Siva is an experienced policeman who is extremely impressed by the intelligence he sees in Sherlock Sam. He loves kaya toast and coffee from Chin Mee Chin, a bakery in Katong.

LUIS ALVARADO
Luis is ten years old and in the fourth grade at Enterprise International School. An expert in Four Square, Luis loves sports and the beach. Originally from California, Luis has grown to love Singaporean culture and food, especially Milo.

FIDEL ALVARADO
Fidel worked as a copywriter in the U.S. before moving to Singapore. He started writing children's books because he wanted to encourage his son to read more. Fidel loves wearing hats and drinking *kopi c peng* (Singaporean iced coffee with evaporated milk).

MARIA OLGA ALVARADO
Maria Olga works long hours and is happy that Fidel is able to write from home and spend time with Luis. When she's free, she'll make delicious Mexican food for her family. She collects tiny bottles from around the world.

ACTIVITY 1
Four Square

I can't believe that Samuel Tan Cher Lock and his friends don't know how to play Four Square. It's so simple. I'm Eliza, by the way, if you haven't already figured it out.

Four Square originated on U.S. elementary school playgrounds and is played on a square court divided into four smaller, equal squares. All you need are a ball the size of a basketball (it has to be able to bounce—a kickball is perfect) and chalk to draw the four squares and number them clockwise 1, 2, 3, 4. Choose a player to be in Square 1 in any way you like. I normally play rock, paper, scissors because I win every time—I'm good at that game, too.

The basic rules:

1. Bounce the ball into an opponent's square such that it bounces out without he or she being able to catch it.

2. The ball cannot bounce in a player's square twice. If that happens, that player is out. REMEMBER THIS!

3. When someone is out, everyone else (usually me because I'm really good at this game) moves up a square and a new player will enter the game. Still don't understand? It's super simple! If a player in Square 3 is out, the player in Square 4 will move up a square to Square 3, leaving Square 4 empty. The players in Square 1 and 2 stay put. The new player will enter in Square 4. Remember, always move up a square, not down!

Next, we have optional rules. Any player who breaks these rules is automatically out. Also, only the player in Square 1 is allowed to add in rules before serving the ball.

Examples of optional rules:

1. **Whirlpool:** The ball must be passed clockwise or counterclockwise until the player in Square 1 or Square 2 says, "End whirlpool!"

2. **No Returns:** Players are not allowed to bounce the ball into the square of the person who just passed it to them.

3. **No Holding:** Players are not allowed to catch and hold the ball, but must instead quickly bounce it to another square.

Remember, these are just a few examples. There are many more optional rules, and you can make up your own rules as you learn the game. I like to make up my own rules all the time.

Simple, right? Anyone can join or leave the game whenever they feel like. For example, Sherlock leaves often to get himself a chicken wing. If you need more help, you can go to *sherlocksam.wordpress.com* and click on "FUN!" for more details.

What are you waiting for? Go play Four Square now!

Hello, everybody! Sherlock Sam here! I learned how to make *horchata* from Uncle Fidel and Auntie Maria Olga recently, and I have decided to share the recipe with you! It's a very cooling summer drink, and the ingredients can be found pretty much all over the world! You won't have to go to any specialty shops or anything!

This recipe makes enough for six people to drink, but if you want to scale up or down, just use maths! If you would like to make enough for twelve people, then double your ingredients. If you would like to make enough for only three people, then halve your ingredients. I might show up at your house while solving a mystery one day, so you should definitely have enough for me, just in case!

You will need the following ingredients:

1 cup uncooked white long-grain rice
5 cups water
½ cup milk
½ tablespoon vanilla extract
¾ teaspoon ground cinnamon
⅔ cup white sugar

First, you will need to pour all the rice and water into a blender. A coffee grinder can work as well. Blend only until the rice begins to break up, which should be about a minute with most blenders. Once that's done, let the rice water mixture stand at room temperature for at least three hours. Go do some homework, solve a mystery, or eat lunch. If you're like me, you'll be able to do all three!

Once the three hours have passed, strain the rice water into a container of your choice, and discard the rice. It's okay if some of the rice gets through. Uncle Fidel and Auntie Maria Olga say some people leave all the rice in. Stir the milk, vanilla, cinnamon, and sugar into the container with the rice water, and then put this in your refrigerator overnight. Yes, you have to wait overnight. It won't taste as good if you try to drink immediately, so go put your pajamas on and read some Batman or Sherlock Holmes. Or one of my adventures!

The next morning, you will need to stir your *horchata* immediately before serving so that the cinnamon is evenly distributed. It tends to settle after a while. Uncle Fidel and Auntie Maria Olga say *horchata* is best when there are ice cubes in your cup, so remember to keep it cool!

And that's it! You've made your very own *horchata*! Remember to always keep some handy, in case I come over!

ACTIVITY 3
Word Search!

I'm Jimmy! Sherlock gave me this puzzle to do, but I can't find all the words! Can you help me? We need to look really, really hard: up, down, sideways, backward, forward, diagonally, upside down, and sideways. Wait, did I say sideways already? These tricky words could be anywhere! Ready? Set? GO!

Words:

- ❏ BRAS BASAH COMPLEX
- ❏ CARROT CAKE
- ❏ CHAIN MAIL
- ❏ CHICKEN WING
- ❏ CLUES
- ❏ ENTERPRISE
- ❏ FOUNTAIN PEN
- ❏ HOLOGRAM
- ❏ HORCHATA
- ❏ MISPOSITIONED
- ❏ QUALITY PAPER
- ❏ SHERLOCK
- ❏ TACO
- ❏ WATSON

```
Q U A R I Y T I L M A R G L L P O S I T S
T X M E L L G N I W N E K C I H C R O H B
M I S P O S I T I O N E D C A R R O C R M
A B C A I N L I A N E S C H A I N M A I L
R R P P R E T N E L P T R A C O E S E C W
G A R Y A T A H C L N P A X O C B E M H I
O H Q T P L E X R R I S E C C A K E F I N
L B U I I C S E P I A S K Y S L C U E L S
O A A L L N I W H A T S O A S E U L C E O
H S L A O O R P I N N S H E R L O C K S N
O A I U C S P L C H U C A C H I L F S R T
L S T Q K T R E L H O R C H A T A O B E A
O U R A C A E X T M F R O S H E Q U A L I
Q O C A Y W T S P A C O C Y K C M N B L N
H A P S T Y N L S A C O M P L I X T A E S
K E K C O L E K A C T O R R A C O C I N T
R A M I S X P O S I T C A R R T C A K O A
C H I L S R E L L N O S O R C H A T E S W
```

ABOUT THE AUTHORS

A.J. Low is a husband-and-wife writing team!

Adan Jimenez was born in the San Joaquin Valley in California to Mexican immigrant parents. He became an immigrant himself when he moved to Singapore after living in New York for almost a decade. He has worked for comic book stores, bookstores, gaming stores, and even a hoagie sandwich shop once. He loves comics, LEGOs, books, games (analog and video), *Doctor Who*, and sandwiches.

Felicia Low-Jimenez has been a geeky bookseller for most of her adult life. She has bought books, sold books, marketed books, and now she is trying her hand at writing books. She loves to nap and eat chocolate. She spends most of her free time reading, and, when she can afford it, she travels, usually to look for beautiful bookstores around the world.

Sherlock Sam and the Missing Heirloom in Katong won the International Schools Libraries Network's Red Dot Award 2013–2014 in the Younger Readers' Category. *Sherlock Sam and the Ghostly Moans in Fort Canning* took third place in the Popular Readers' Choice Awards 2013 in the English Children's Books category.

You can find them at *sherlocksam.wordpress.com*, *facebook.com/ SherlockSamSeries*, and *sherlock.sam.sg@gmail.com*.

ABOUT THE ILLUSTRATOR

Andrew Tan (also known as drewscape) is a full-time freelance illustrator and an Eisner-nominated comic artist. He illustrates for print ads and magazines, and also enjoys storyboarding and illustrating for picture book projects. During his free time, he creates his own comics for the fun of it. In his home studio you'll find an overflow of art tools of all kinds as he loves experimenting with them. He already has too many fountain pens and tells himself that he will stop buying more. Andrew published his first graphic novel, *Monsters, Miracles & Mayonnaise*, in 2012.